Dino Park

Adapted by Lauren Forte
Based on the episode "Dino Park" written b

Cover design by Elaine Lopez-Levine.

Little, Brown and Company
Hachette Book Group
1290 Avenue of the Americas, New York, NY 10104
Visit us at lb-kids.com
bobthebuilder.com

First Edition: July 2017

LB kids is an imprint of Little, Brown and Company.
The LB kids name and logo are trademarks of Hachette Book Group, Inc.

The publisher is not responsible for websites (or their content) that are not owned by the publisher.

Library of Congress Control Number 2016911318

ISBN 978-0-316-54814-4

Printed in the United States of America

CW

10 9 8 7 6 5 4 3 2 1

Bob, Muck, Scoop, and Lofty were at the entrance to Fixham's brand-new Dino Park.

"Mayor Madison has asked for a private preview of the exhibits tonight," Bob said. "She wants to see the life-sized models of the dinosaurs before the new Dino Park opens to the public."

"Good thing the dinosaurs are arriving today," Scoop said.

"How many dinosaurs will there be?" asked Lofty.

"There will be five," Bob answered as he scrolled through some pictures on his tablet. "An ankylosaurus, an iguanodon, a stegosaurus, a pterodactyl, and there'll be one special triceratops that can move and roar!"

"So...lots of dinosaurs are coming?" Muck asked nervously.

"The dinosaurs are only models," Leo said. "Don't be scared."

Muck wasn't convinced. "I don't think I like dinosaurs," he replied.

"Actually, when I was a little kid, I was a bit frightened of them, too," Leo said. "But I got over it by pretending to roar like a dinosaur as loudly as I could. Try it, Muck."

"Okay," Muck murmured. He took a deep breath, opened his mouth, and...*"RAAAAAAAAAHHHHHHHHHH!"*

"That sounded fierce!" Leo exclaimed. "Do you feel better?"

"A little bit," Muck admitted. "Thanks, Leo."

Meanwhile, back at the park entrance, Two-Tonne arrived with a huge dinosaur on his trailer.

"Wow!" shouted Scoop. "Which dinosaur is this, Bob?"

"This is the iguanodon," Bob answered.

Two-Tonne chuckled. "And there are lots more to come!"

He still had four more dinosaurs to deliver!

After the dinosaurs had been delivered, Lofty moved the triceratops into position. Scoop and Bob followed behind to help.

"Okay, Lofty," Bob called. "Slowly lower it down and then carefully release it."

Once the model was on the ground, Bob attached it to a power cable.

"Great!" he called. "Now to test it."

Scoop and Lofty watched carefully, waiting for the dinosaur to do something.

"It's not moving," Scoop said in a disappointed voice.

"The triceratops has built-in detectors," Bob explained. "It will only move when someone gets close to it. Try it, Scoop."

Scoop approached the model, and when he got close enough, the triceratops burst to life! It raised its head, shook it from side to side, opened its mouth, and let out a loud *ROOOOOAAAAARRR!*

"Ooooooh," **Scoop said. He couldn't believe how scary the triceratops model was! It sounded like a real dinosaur!**

Scoop and Lofty wanted to play a joke. When Bob walked away for a moment, Scoop moved the triceratops into the middle of the road.

Bob returned just as Leo and Muck were coming around the corner.

"Remember, Muck," Leo said, still trying to reassure him. "These dinosaurs are not real."

"If you say so, Leo," Muck replied.

But as Muck finished coming around the bend, he rolled right into a scary, roaring dinosaur!

"Arghhhhh!" Muck shouted. "The dinosaur's alive! Take cover!"

Muck wanted to be brave, so he charged at the triceratops.

"No, stop! Don't!" shouted Bob and Leo.

But Muck couldn't hear them. He knocked the model through a wooden fence and sent it tumbling over a cliff!

"Oh, Muck," Bob said with a sigh. "What have you done?"

"I'm sorry, Bob. I forgot that it was only a model," Muck said sadly. "I thought it was real. It definitely sounded real!"

Scoop and Lofty felt bad for trying to play a joke. "We're sorry, Bob. We just wanted to surprise everyone."

"But now we've lost the Dino Park's main attraction," Bob said with a groan.

"And there isn't much time before Mayor Madison arrives!" Leo added.

Scoop peered over the edge of the cliff. “The triceratops is only halfway down,” he said. “And it’s still in one piece!”

“*Hmm*...if we can reach it, we can still get the park finished in time,” Bob replied.

“But how?” Lofty asked. “It’s a long way down.”

“I’ll rappel down the cliff!” Bob exclaimed.

Bob strapped on his rappel harness and gave the team instructions.

"Okay, Scoop. You'll be my anchor," he said. "So you need to stay still and keep your brakes on."

"Understood, Bob!" Scoop agreed.

"Lofty," added Bob, "you lower your hook when I call you from the ledge."

"You got it, Bob," Lofty promised.

Bob carefully rappelled down the side of the cliff. When Bob got to the triceratops, Lofty lowered his hook so Bob could attach it to the straps around the dinosaur.

"Take us up, Lofty!" Bob called.

"Bob's a dinosaur-riding cowboy!" Muck declared.

"We did it!" Lofty cheered.

"It's not over yet," said Bob. "We need to hurry and get the park finished! CAN WE BUILD IT?"

"YES, WE CAN!" cheered the team.

Everyone immediately got to work.

Bob repaired the broken fence by the cliff's edge.

Lofty lifted the pterodactyl model into place.

Leo hammered signs in front of all the dinosaurs.

Soon Mayor Madison and her right-hand man, Mr. Bentley, were waiting at the gates. Bob ran to greet them.

"Mayor Madison, we're ready for your visit to the Dino Park."

"Excellent, Bob," said the mayor. "I'm so looking forward to seeing it—especially the prized triceratops."

"As am I," added Mr. Bentley. "I'm just glad you've finished the park on schedule."

The group toured the park.

"Very impressive!" announced Mayor Madison as they passed the iguanodon.

"Oh, that's brilliant! Fantastic!" she exclaimed after seeing the pterodactyl.

As they arrived at the triceratops, it moved and reared its head! It looked very ferocious, but it didn't roar.

"*Hmm*, isn't it meant to make a sound?" the mayor asked.

Muck, who was parked off to the side, realized that the fall over the cliff must have broken the model's roar. So he took a deep breath, opened his mouth, and...

"RAAAAAAAAAHHHHHHHHHHH!" he bellowed.

Muck's roar was so ferocious that even Bob and his team hid in the trees!

Muck was very pleased with himself. He'd helped save the day, and he'd conquered his fear of dinosaurs. "I like pretending to be a dinosaur!" he declared.